LIBERTY AND BEAREMY'S
ADVENTURES 🐾 IN 🐾
NEW YORK

ISBN 978-1-68526-310-2 (Paperback)
ISBN 978-1-68526-311-9 (Digital)

Covenant Books
11661 Hwy 707
Murrells Inlet, SC 29576
www.covenantbooks.com

LIBERTY AND BEAREMY'S

ADVENTURES

IN

NEW YORK

The Statue of Liberty

Ashley Stoner

Liberty put on her favorite New York shirt.
Well, really the only one she had.
She pulled up her skinny jeans
that were hugging her just a tad.

Bearemy threw on his favorite hoodie,
showing his favorite place.
Yes, it said, "I love New York,"
and put the biggest smile on his face.

He put on his denim leg by leg.
It was a different color and design.
His fit a little looser than hers,
if he only had a belt his size.

For her, being his little sister,
he always got teased
because she was always taller than him
by an inch or two or three.

Liberty and Bearemy brushed all their fur,
making sure they looked just right.
They were looking forward to walking
the streets of New York
throughout the day and night.

They went to the Statue of Liberty
and climbed all 354 steps to the crown.

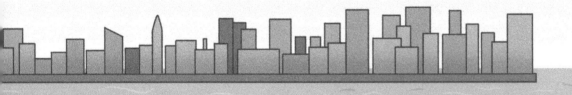

They looked out at the glorious view
and forgot they had to come down.

Holding on to the rail
and hugging the winding stairs,
they gradually made it down
and were thankful they were just bears.

They boarded the ferry to go back
to visit the city some more.
Liberty wanted to get some fruit,
so they thought they'd stop by the store.

On the way to the store,
they saw a farmer's stand.
Liberty bought some bananas.
They seemed to be in high demand.

21

After riding on the subway
and getting off at Times Square,
they saw so many people
that they've seen anywhere.

While walking down the street,
they thought they'd like to see a show.
They got some discount tickets
for seats up in the fourth row.

They had never been on Broadway
to see a musical or a play.
The moment for them was magical,
the end to a fabulous day!

About the Author

Ashley is a Kansas girl but loves to travel to other states and countries. Her favorite state she has been to is New York, and she has relived some of her adventures she has had with her mom in the form of teddy bears.

CPSIA information can be obtained
at www.ICGtesting.com
Printed in the USA
LVHW071959270922
729405LV00006B/182

9 781685 263102